Puppy Scents
The Kids' Guide to Puppy Care
Narrated by Roc Weiler

Written by Don Kaleta • Illustrated by Helen Habel

Dedication

This book is dedicated to moms & dads, boys & girls and dog owners everywhere. Puppies are like kids. They are only little for a brief time. Have fun with your puppy, learn why they do what they do and know that understanding each other is not only key to making friends with your new pup, but is also important in all your relationships in life. Give your pup kindness, love, respect and leadership and you will have a dog who not only loves you, but is happy to be your friend forever. – Don Kaleta

Acknowledgements

I would especially like to give my heartfelt thanks to my wife Mindy for her uncountable hours spent in research, editing, encouragement and support. It has been a wild and wonderful ride. All my gratitude and love. – Don

Thanks to my husband Mark, sons James and Ben, neighbor Brandon, and our cat Smokey for their encouragement, support and willingness to help out when needed. – Helen

Published and distributed in the United States by Kaleta Publishing, LLC
Contact mindyjkaleta@gmail.com

Design and Editorial Assistance: Phoenix Graphix Design and Publishing Services

Library of Congress Control Number: 2010912818
ISBN: 978-0-615-39881-5

1st Edition/Printing 2010
Printed in USA

BookMasters, Inc.
30 Amberwood Parkway, Ashland, OH. 44805
Job# M7810
September 2010

A Pup's Story

A Note to Parents from Don…

You hold in your hand *The Kids' Guide to Puppy Care* that came from information in the e-book, *Surviving the Puppy Stage, How to Get Inside Your Dog's Mind Without Losing Your Own*, the parents' guide by my wife, Mindy J Kaleta.

Puppy Scents, The Kids' Guide to Puppy Care is written from the dog's point of view. With the pup's thoughts, feelings and suggestions on training, kids begin to understand that their puppy is not so different from themselves.

Our wish is that both you and your children enjoy the little pup's story and come away feeling delighted and eager to train, love and bond with your new puppy. Training is a family thing. Enjoy!

Hey, don't forget to look for the parents' e-book guide!

Available online everywhere!

How It All Started...

Yep! It happened to me just like it has to a lot of other pups.

There I was, playing nip and tag with my brothers and sisters in a box in the front yard, when all of a sudden a shadow came over us. "Oh no," I said. "I hope it's not a rain cloud. We are having so much fun."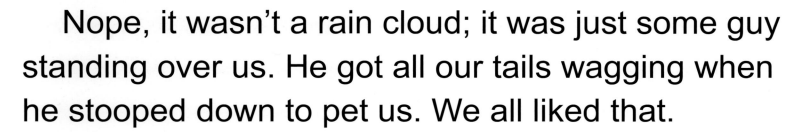

Nope, it wasn't a rain cloud; it was just some guy standing over us. He got all our tails wagging when he stooped down to pet us. We all liked that.

When he got to me he said that I had a personality all my own. I'm thinking to myself, a *personality*? Maybe it will come off and go away as I get older.

He got me a little scared. But he picked me up, and scratched me behind my ears. Oh, that felt sooo good. Then he put me down on the grass so we could play. I licked him and I let him scratch my belly too. That felt *really* good.

Then he said those magic words, "How about coming home with me?"

Yipppeee! You bet! The box was getting a little small for all of us anyway, and someone bit my tail the last time we were playing.

This guy had a nice smile and kind eyes. He just looked like someone I needed to go home with and take care of. After all, maybe that's why I'm here. I've got a feeling he *really* needs me.

Home Coming

After I decided to go home with him, I said good-bye to my brothers, sisters and the nice people who took care of me.

The people said to the man, "Don, you've got one great pup there, and we're sure you'll be the best of friends always." All I got out of that is, I'm going to my new home with this nice guy and his name is Don. Woohoo, Don, let's go!

Don put me in this boxy suitcase, then carried me to his red truck. Wow, let the adventure begin!

When we got to the truck, he put me on the floor so I wouldn't be scared. Good idea! I *was* scared a little bit, but didn't want to show him.

We weren't in the truck long before we stopped and he said, "Your home now, little buddy." Oh, boy! Oh, boy! Oh, boy! I'm sooo excited! Let's get out of here.

Well, he picked up my box and carried me to the back yard. He opened the door on my box and I shot out like a rocket. There were so many new things to smell. That's how we pups get to know things; we smell them. I guess its **Puppy Scents**!

Come and Get It

After checking out my new back yard, Don took me in the house to show me around. Soon we were in the kitchen, and I heard Don messing around with a bag.

Wait a minute. I know that smell. Hey! I smell food. I hope it's for me. All that exploring and chasing critters in my new back yard really made me hungry. This being a pup is hard work.

Don said, "Well, little buddy, are you hungry?" And I was thinking, "You bet, I'm starving! Yoohooo, Don! Do you see me? Oh, boy, Oh, boy! He sees me and he's bringing something to put in my new, shiny bowl!"

Well, I gobbled it down as fast as I could so I would get my share. But then I noticed I didn't have to fight for my food anymore. It was all mine. Cool…

Don was telling me that since I'm a pup, he'd be giving me snacks all day. No big meals… until I'm bigger. I'm only about ten weeks old, so he gives me three to four meals a day. And that's okay with me! Just keep them coming, yummy!

When & Where

Since I got my little tummy filled up and drank some water, I really had to go potty.

Don put a leash on my collar and took me out to the back yard to what must have been a special place because he said, "Here, little buddy, this is where you need to do your business."

Well, I don't know what that word *business* means but I knew what I had to do. Go potty! Puppies have to go potty a lot. You just have to remember this. If you even think we might need to go potty, we do.

Oh, one more thing. Dogs have to find the right spot to go potty. Don takes me to my potty area, but he gives me time to find that right spot. Hey! It's important. I don't know why we need to do this, we just do. Give us time. We'll find it.

A Place of My Own

After I went potty, we went back into the house and Don said, "Are you tired, little buddy? Maybe it's time for a nap." I didn't want to show him I was pooped, so I'm glad he read my mind. I was ready for a nap.

Well, he set up an area in the corner of his house for me. In fact, I have my own, *yes*, my own little house. I guess it's really called a crate. But it's home to me.

It's just big enough, with a blanket on the floor and a couple of neat toys in it. It even has a door. Boy! Am I moving up in the world. Somebody take my picture. I want to send it to my brothers and sisters.

When Don put me in my house, he closed the door and said, "You have a nice little nap now, little buddy." That sounded great. But it was hard to do. I missed my brothers and sisters snuggling around me to keep me warm. So, I guess I got a little whiny.

Don heard me crying and came back to see what was the matter. He said, "Oh, I think I know what the problem is. You miss the warmth of your family. I've got an idea."

So, he got this thing called a hot water bottle. He wrapped it up in my blanket, and that felt ohhhh, so good. Boy, that worked just fine.

I lay next to it, I got under it and then on top of it. I liked the top best. It worked great. I guess I'm still trying to get used to being by myself. But it's kind of neat.

Having a place of my own keeps me from getting into trouble when Don can't watch me.

He does check on me often to see if I'm okay or if I need to go potty. He knows that I don't want to make a mess in my house. That would be nasty and stinky. Not fun for either one of us.

A Game Called "Focus"

I learned a new game today called, "Focus." And you know what? It involved treats! And I Love Treats!

Anyhoo, this is how the game is played. My pal Don told me to sit in front of him. Then he said, "Focus," while he was holding my treat close to his lips. I'm thinking to myself, "Hey, that's my treat!"

I just sat and stared at him. I guess that's where the "focus" comes in: sitting long enough to pay attention. He counted to five and gave me my treat. I like this game. Let's play again.

So we did, over and over. I would get excited, jump around, and Don would say, "Sit," again, and I did. Then he would say, "Focus," and I did. He counted to five and then it was treat time again. Yummy!

Besides learning to focus, I think I'm learning to count. 1, 2, 3, 4, 5… and that's it.

I thought I did pretty good playing this game. The only thing I couldn't keep still was my tail. Sometimes, it just has a mind of its own. I'll look back at it, and there it is wiggling and waving around, daring me to chase it. So, I do. But doggone it's fast! But one of these days…

Anyhow, after we had finished, Don said, "Okay, all done." That means it's recess and you know all kids love recess almost as much as treats. Well… almost.

What a Ride!

Let's talk about taking rides in the car. I just want to clue you in on something. I'm not that much different than all kids. If you just take me places I don't really like, such as the doctor to get a shot, I won't want to go. And it may take some time on your part to get me back into the car. C'mon, would you?

Take your pup to some fun places also, like to your ballgames, the car wash or for a picnic in the park. We will even ride along to the post office. We just like being with you and doing fun stuff.

29

I've talked to some of my backyard pals, and not all of us like taking a ride. Some are scared and like to sit on the floor and not look out the windows. Some like to be in their crate where they feel safe. But me, I like to have the window down just far enough for me to have that fresh air blow right into my nose. Oh, what a rush!

But don't allow us pups to stick our heads outside the window. We might like how that feels, but there is always a chance that we might get something in our eyes or we may get so excited that we'll jump out. And that would be a bad thing. We might get hurt.

One more thing to remember – NEVER leave us pups alone longer than five minutes in the car. Always leave the window opened a little bit. It's really scary for us, and dangerous, especially in hot weather. We want to go everywhere with you. Make it safe and fun.

My Trip to the Park

Now this was fun! One day Don took me for a ride in the truck to a place called a dog park.

When we got there, Don put me on my leash. We walked over to a big area that was fenced in, went in through the gate, then he took off my leash and said, "Go play!" Are you kidding me? You don't have to tell me twice!

There were all kinds of dogs there, kids like me and some grownup dogs too. I wanted to meet everyone, and I think they were excited to meet me. That was so much fun.

I ran, jumped around, climbed on things and did a whole bunch of sniffin' around. Don just watched me and once in a while he'd call my name and say, "Come." So, I would, because I love my pal and we always have a good time together. Then he'd pat me all over, say I was a good boy, give me a treat and then say, "Go play!"

Out of my way! I'm off to play some more. We did this quite a few times. He'd call my name, say, "Come," and I'd come, get praised, patted and a treat. Life is good!

I heard Don telling another man at the park that teaching your dog to come is so very important. If you only call us when you want to go home, or to stop having fun, or to do something that's not that pleasant, we won't want to come. So, you have to mix up the reasons. Then we never know if we're getting something good, or if we really do need to go home. But we'll come anyway. It works best for all of us. And there just might be a treat!

And you know, I love treats!

Let's Party!

Can I let you in on a secret? I overheard my new pal, Don, talking to his friend and he said he was going to give me a party. Oh, how exciting! He said it's his way of introducing me to his family, friends and neighbors. Oh, my goodness! What should I wear? I can't wait!

Hey, everyone could use some free "pup-plicity." Get it? Oh, sorry, I think Don's scents, I mean *sense* of humor is rubbing off on me.

He said it's really important that I learn to meet all different types of people and animals. That's okie-dokie with me. There's going to be balloons, streamers, party hats, kids, grownups and I'm hoping, lots of treats.

Don said that being around all kinds of people and other animals will help me to learn how to behave with them. I don't care; I'll do it.

My party day was so much fun. They played a game called Meet the Puppy – that's me. It seemed like everybody wanted to hold me, and why not, I'm sooo cute they couldn't help themselves.

This one really nice lady at my party picked me up and said, "Hello. Aren't you a sweet puppy." Then she began to check out my paws, my ears and opened my mouth to look at my teeth. She kept giving me treats the whole time I was on her lap.

Then she turned me over on my back and rubbed my belly and said, "What a nice little boy." Then she gave me a big hug.

Good golly, I really like this lady. Of course, it has nothing to do with the treats she's giving me. Of course not. Did I tell you I really like treats? And the hug was pretty good too.

I heard her say to the little girl sitting next to her that gently handling a pup like this will make a visit to a vet or groomer more fun. Maybe they'll have treats too. I hope so. Party on!

Taking Don for a Walk

On our first try to go outside for a walk, I couldn't wait. Don put my leash on me and instantly I thought I was a snow puppy pulling a sled. I thought it was a blast, but Don didn't. He said something about his arm and a socket? I don't know what he meant by that, but he wasn't too excited about me taking *him* for a walk. Must be a human thing.

Well, this is how we worked things out so we could walk calmly together.

This time he had me sit next to him on his left side, and then he said, "Let's go." We walked a little bit and then he stopped and said, "Sit." It took me a few times until I realized that when he walked, he wanted me to walk. When he stopped, he wanted me to sit.

But he was really smart to keep doing it over and over until I got it. He never got mad at me if I didn't do it just right. He would just say, "Let's go," and we'd try again. It was as simple as that. Even a pup can understand it.

If I got too excited, he would just change directions and keep walking as if to teach me that I had to keep paying attention or get left behind.

I'm thinking all along, if this goes well, there's got to be a treat for me. And sure enough there was and a lot of praise when I did things his way. We dogs love to be praised. Gotta love us!

Oh, almost forgot to mention this. Sometimes, while we're walking along, I'll have to go potty… you know, the stinky one. Well, it's a natural thing and Don knows this. So, he brings along a plastic bag to clean up what I did. He says it's the right thing to do and people will always like us for not leaving a mess for them to clean up or step in later. Yuck!

Yippee! You're Home!

One day as I was busy chewing on one of my toys, I looked up and Don was gone. I wondered where he went. Then all of a sudden, I heard someone at the door. It's Don! He's home!

"Oh, boy, you're home! Good golly, I missed you!" So I jumped up to get close to Don's face to show him how glad I was to see him. But he wasn't too happy. He told me to get "off." I didn't understand. What did he mean, "Off"? Why shouldn't I jump up to see him? Look how adorable I am! I just wanted to say hello.

But Don made it clear that people don't want pups to jump up on them to say hello.

That must be where the "off" comes in. He said we needed to work on meeting people nicely at the door.

But I don't mind. I want to learn the right way to say hello so people don't get mad at me and not want to come back to see me.

Okay, so I was wondering what *should* I do when someone is at the door? Don said, "Let's play a little game." He said that he would go outside and act like he's coming in again. Okie-dokie. This will be fun.

So, Don goes outside, rings the doorbell. I hear the door opening. Yippee! Don's home again! I want to get closer to his face to say hello, but this time he says, "Sit." I know "sit," so I do. I got a pat on the head and a treat. Yes, I said treat. And you know how much I love those treats!

Well, we worked on this a few times, I didn't always get a treat, but there was always a chance I would, so I just did what he asked. We even practiced me greeting family and friends too. Sitting to say hello is a great way to show how well behaved I am. It makes me look like a smarty-pants, and makes them like me even more. Hey, I'm game!

I'm Not Really Part Beaver (or Am I?)

Man, oh, man, did I mention another thing I love to do? Well, that's chewing. I can't help myself. Chewing makes my teeth and gums feel so good.

Don told his pals I'm in the teething stage now. I don't know exactly what that means, but I sure like chewing on pretty much anything. So, if you don't want me to nibble on it, you'd better hide it away.

Guess it's a part of me growing up. I like to chew on both hard and soft toys. For a change from toys, I really like ice cubes and dog biscuits. They are good too.

But be careful what you let me chew on. If you allow me to chew on any of your old socks or old shoes, I won't know the difference between an old sock and a new one, or an old leather shoe or your new leather couch. And if I chew on something

that's not mine, I'm going to get into trouble. And hey, that's not fair. I don't know. You need to show me. I'm just a pup. A wise, old dog said once, "I am what I am." And I am a pup. And proud of it!

Just a Little Nip

Puppies bite. That's just what we do. It's natural. No hands, right? We have to get your attention somehow. Biting is how we learn, explore and have fun.

Don was telling one of his friends that a puppy who does not learn that biting or nipping hurts can have trouble as a grownup and could really hurt someone.

Tell us when we are biting too hard. Say, "Oww!" or "Ouch!" really loud to let us know how much it hurts you. We won't know that it hurts if you don't tell us.

We pups really don't want to hurt anyone. We're just playing. So let us know when we are playing too rough.

If we are too excited to listen, a good way to stop us is to walk away to another room and shut the door. It keeps you safe and we pups have lost our playmate. Give us some time, we will calm down and then we can play again soon. We will be better playmates as we learn and get older. Just be patient with us. We'll grow out of it.

Who's the Boss?

I'm going to let you in on a little secret. Don't tell any other pups I told you this. Puppies like to do what they want. If we can get away with anything, we will. It's a kid thing! But in the dog world, there has to be a leader that we can trust to take care of us.

Just between you and me, I'm beginning to trust Don more and more. I usually don't get into trouble if I let him be the boss. Go figure.

So, do us pups a favor. You be the boss. Show us that we can trust you to take care of us.

Here are a few things you can do to help when working with your puppy.

Use a regular voice when telling us what to do. Don't yell or scream. Remember we're just pups and you'll scare us. Speak in a medium, firm tone.

Food treats always work to help us pups learn to listen. We're easy.

🦴 If we happen to eat about the same time, you eat first, you're the boss and bosses eat first.

🦴 You always lead the way, no matter where we go. It's best we follow you. It's just another way of showing who's the leader. And you are the leader of your pup.

If we work on these things together, life is going to be sooooo good.

Calm Down

While Don and I were working on training, it was time for recess. I like recess. Not as much as I like treats, but pretty close.

Anyway, we started chasing each other around the yard, wrestling, playing ball and go fetch. I was really starting to get the hang of that game when Don said, "Calm down." Well, that was really hard to do. Oh, man! I wanted to keep playing.

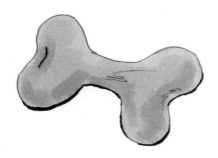

It took me a little while because I get pretty crazy when we're playing. But I soon did settle down. When I did, Don patted me and said I was his good boy and kept talking to me in a calm voice. That really did help me to settle down. Then he got all excited again and said, "Okay! Go Play!"

Are you kidding me? All right, let's go! We did this a lot of times, and sometimes I'd even get a treat. I think what he was teaching me is that at times I'll

have to calm down really fast. It doesn't mean we're done playing, just taking a recess. We will play again soon.

I'm trying really hard to make puppy scents, I mean *sense*, of what Don does with me. But I trust him and there's always a chance there just might be a treat in it for me.

Did I tell you? I know, you know. But I'm going tell you anyway…
I Love Treats!!!

About Those Treats

Okay. So, by now you know that… I LOVE TREATS!

But… I have to be fair here. Don did give me a lot of treats, especially when I first came home with him. But as I began to learn and am getting a little older, he stopped giving me treats for every little thing I do… BUMMER!

At first I was mad about that, but it turned out okay, because instead of a food treat, he would switch to a toy or praise and lots of hugs. I really like those too!

I guess the bottom line is a pudgy pet is not a healthy pet. So, watch what you give us pups, we'll eat just about anything. And don't give us human food. It makes our tummies fat and makes us slow when we are trying to run.

So remember: Just use good **Puppy Scents** when taking care of your pup. And your pup will live a long, happy life with you.

Guess Who?

Well, if you haven't guessed by now who the pup in this story is, it's me, Roc Weiler!

I'm not that little pup anymore, but I'm still learning and so is Don. He says you are never too old to stop learning. And we have a whole lot more to learn together.

The reason I wrote this book is that I want you to be the best pal you can be to your new pup; just like Don is for me!

Love and care for us, just like we're your new brother or sister. We depend on you!

As I'm watching TV and hear stories of pets being dropped off somewhere all alone, not being treated very nicely or going without food and water, it makes me sad.

My brothers, sisters and I had a rough start also. We were left all alone with no one to care for us. We got very lucky when people from an animal shelter found us. They took really good care of us, and found us nice homes with families like yours. So, if you are just planning on getting a pup and don't have one yet, check out your local shelters, humane societies or go to an online site like www.Petfinder.com. That perfect pal is just waiting for you.

I also want to thank Don for helping me write this book. I would have written it myself but it's kind of hard when  you… have no hands! Hey! But I can run faster than him!

It's been fun telling you my story. Just remember, have patience while we get through puppyhood, it will go by really fast. Maybe I'll write another book for you when I'm older, we'll see. So long for now!

Your pal, Roc

Puppies Rule!

About the author, Don Kaleta, and the narrator, Roc

Don is a regular guy who loves helping people. As a young retiree with 36 years of service with AT&T, he now works in a nursing and rehabilitation center in Columbus, Ohio, where he fills up his days keeping a pleasant and safe environment for residents and staff.

Due to his inability to be nothing other than a kid in a grownup body, Puppy Scents, The Kids' Guide to Puppy Care was born. His out-of-the-ordinary sense of humor and quirky way of looking at life is evident in the writing of this book.

Don is the proud father of three adult boys, Nick, Nathan and Jason, and lives in the small town of Pataskala, Ohio, with his wife Mindy, and shares their home with their three cats and Roc. Don can be contacted through:

www.puppy-scents.com

Roc was born in the state of Virginia and found his way to a local shelter along with six of his siblings, and all were lucky enough to be adopted. Roc found his new home with Don and Mindy in May of 2010 at the young age of ten weeks. He is constantly adding chapters to his story. To see what Roc is up to lately, visit his blog on www.Puppy-Scents.com or join his Facebook page, Puppy-Scents.

About the illustrator, Helen Habel, artist and instructor of Captured Essence

As a child Helen was always sketching every spare minute she had and knew someday that she would illustrate children's books. Now with the help of Don Kaleta's imagination and her artistic abilities, her childhood dream has come true.

Helen also enjoys relaxing with oil paints and has been studying under the guidance of renowned artist and instructor Robert Warren in Canal Winchester, Ohio. It was here that she was inspired to always strive to capture the essence of that which she is painting.

Helen works from her studio in Hebron, Ohio, and teaches oil painting classes at various locations as well as in her home studio where she resides with her husband and two sons. Helen can be contacted through:

helenhabel@embarqmail.com

Look for her Facebook page, Captured Essence